THE SEVENTH SISTER

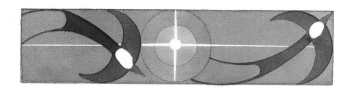

To Mommy and Daddy,
who helped every step of the way—
and to CR
who made sure I got there.

Library of Congress Cataloging-in-Publication Data

Chang, Cindy.
   The seventh sister / retold by Cindy Chang ; illustrated by Charles
Reasoner.
      p.   cm.— (Legends of the world)
   Summary: A lonely shepherd is saddened when he must let the
maiden he loves return to help her sisters weave the tapestry of the
night sky.
   ISBN 0-8167-3411-9 (library)   ISBN 0-8167-3412-7 (pbk.)
   [1. Folklore—China.]   I. Reasoner, Charles, ill.   II. Title.   III. Series.
PZ8.1.C356Se   1994
[398.21]—dc20   93-43179

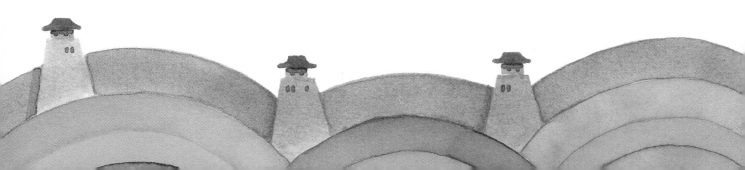

THE SEVENTH SISTER

A CHINESE LEGEND

RETOLD BY CINDY CHANG   ILLUSTRATED BY CHARLES REASONER

TROLL ASSOCIATES

ong ago, in the heavens above, seven beautiful maidens wove the glorious tapestry of the night sky. Each night, celestial magpies spread the tapestry over the earth. But the sun's early rays melted the night, so that day after day, the maidens' nimble fingers had to fly across their looms to complete their task before sunset. They sang as they worked, and their music drifted through the clickety-clack, clickity-clack of their looms.

Though all the sisters were known for their beauty and talent, the youngest, Mei, was the most clever. She made silks finer than the fluffiest clouds, and cloth more colorful than the brightest birds. Yet, even surrounded by the beauty of heaven, Mei was sad and lonely, and her sad song echoed through the sky.

Below, in the grassy lowlands of China, there lived a cowherd named Chang. Every morning, he would rise before the sun and eat a meal of rice porridge and tea. Chang would then begin his long day in the fields, plowing and tilling the soil with his only companion, an ox.

One evening, after a long hot day, Chang rested upon the bank of a small gentle stream. "Even though you are only an ox, you are my closest friend," Chang sighed. "I am not happy, but I do not know what I am missing. Perhaps the answers are in the stars." Then he looked into the sky and filled the air with the sweet, sad songs of his flute.

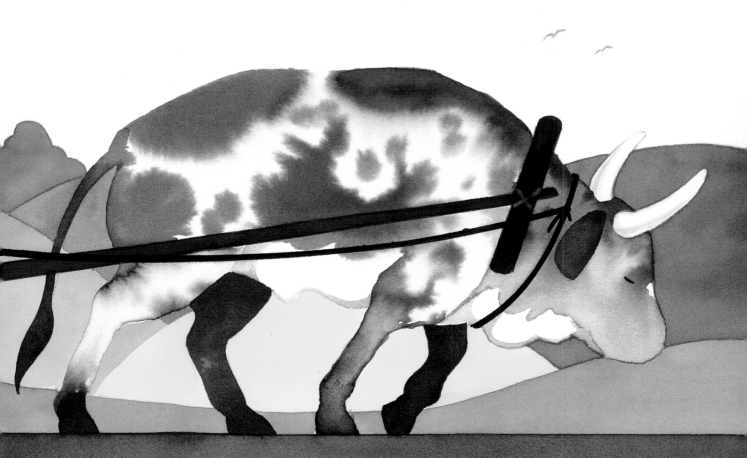

As night fell, the sky turned from blue to lavender and Chang drifted off to sleep. He dreamed that a magpie flew to him and spoke. "Happiness shall be yours, gentle man. Follow the willow trees to the silver pond where the rainbow ends. There, seven maidens gather water to brighten the stars in the sky. The youngest and fairest is Mei. She will remain with you, if you remember one thing. You must hide her magical outer robe, for without it she cannot return to the heavens." With that, the magpie flew away.

Chang awoke with a start. He looked at his ox, resting in the still waters. "I know of no magical ponds," Chang said softly. "Perhaps it is only a silly dream." He patted his ox fondly. "We need to be on the lookout for magical ponds!" laughed Chang as he stared into the night.

The next morning brought a soft, misty rain. Chang set off through the wetness toward a distant field. He passed a small pond shaded from the rain by graceful willow trees. As he stopped to look, the morning's mist began to turn into a rainbow. And beneath the rainbow were seven maidens, chatting and singing.

Each maiden was filling a jar made of moonbeams with water from the pond. And, though each was more lovely than the other, Chang thought the youngest was the fairest of all. "My life would be complete if this fair maiden were part of it," Chang thought.

As he watched, Chang noticed seven robes upon the trees in the distance and remembered his dream. "It is just as the magpie said!" Chang whispered to his ox. Quietly, he grabbed the most delicate robe and hid it.

As the afternoon shadows grew longer, a magpie's song rang through the willows. One by one, the maidens took their outer robes and flew back to their celestial homes. All except for Mei, who looked frantically for hers. Her sisters called for her to hurry. Mei started to cry as she watched her sisters leaving her behind.

Mei's tears were more than Chang's heart could bear. He stepped forward from his hiding place and played a soft song of welcome. Mei smiled at his song, which told of cool, babbling streams and the warm, rising sun. She sang to him about the white sky and her own unhappiness. Soon love songs fluttered about them like butterflies.

he two were so happy, they never noticed that the sun rose earlier than usual the next morning. Mei sent Chang off to work with a kiss, a noon meal of pork and rice wrapped in tea leaves, and a loving scratch for Ox.

The sun was hot. Often, Chang stopped to rest from the scorching heat. His ox moved slowly and finally stopped. Chang looked up at the sun. He knew they had been working all day, yet the sun was no lower than when they had started. "This is very strange," Chang said to the owner of the land.

"The sun is angry," the landowner said. "It is past eight o'clock in the evening, yet the sun does not move. We must have displeased her. But what have we done? What can we do?" Both men scratched their heads in confusion.

hang arrived home to find Mei sipping a cool cup of tea. "Mei, the sun has made it too hot to work. What has made her so angry?"

Mei burst into tears. "It is my fault," she said. "The sun is angry with me."

"What do you mean?" asked Chang.

"Without my help, my sisters have not been able to finish the tapestry of the night sky. The sun has not been able to rest, so she is tired and angry," Mei said with tears streaming down her beautiful face. "I must return."

Chang was quiet as he realized they could not be together. At last, he said in a low voice, "Yes, you must return. Without your work, we will all suffer. You must finish the tapestry of the night sky."

Gently, Chang took Mei's robe from its hiding place and wrapped it around her shoulders. She flew higher and higher into the sky. A flock of magpies accompanied Mei on her journey.

That night, the sun seemed to sink with a grateful sigh as once again the night sky spread across the earth. People slept contentedly, since the sun was no longer angry. But Chang could only sit by the door of his simple hut, filling the night sky with his sweet, sad songs.

Mei returned to her work on the tapestry of the night. Often, she tossed stars across the sky to remind Chang of her love. As she worked, Mei's tears fell onto her loom and became the stars that fill the night sky. So many stars were formed that they became the mighty Milky Way, dividing the sky in two.

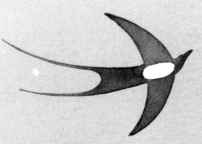

At night, Chang watched the shooting stars and thought of Mei. One night, a magpie came to Chang in a dream. "Happiness shall be yours, gentle man," the magpie said. "The way to Mei is within your reach. Return to the silver pond. There you will find a magpie feather that will take you to Mei. Go quickly, my friend."

Chang awoke and hurried to the pond. There, nestled among the roots of the willows, he saw one lone feather shimmering in the moonlight. Grasping it, he raised his arm and said, "Take me to Mei!" He flew higher and higher into the sky, where Mei was waiting for him.

*B*ut, alas, the vast Milky Way separated Chang from his beloved Mei. "What are we to do now?" cried Chang in despair.

Suddenly a flock of magpies appeared from every corner of the world. As their wings touched, their bodies formed a bridge. Mei and Chang ran lightly across it into each other's waiting arms and their voices rang out in joyous song.

"When you are together, Mei cannot work and all the earth suffers," said the magpie from Chang's dream. "But your love is good and strong, so once a year, we will form a bridge to unite you."

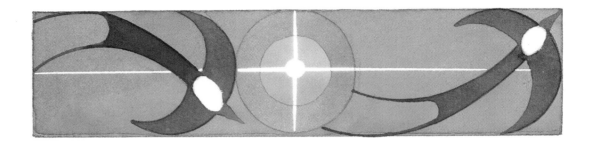

You can still see Chang and Mei in the nighttime sky. On one side of the Milky Way, Mei is a bright star completing the tapestry of the night sky. On the other side, another bright star, the ever-faithful Chang, awaits the seventh day of the seventh month, when he can be with his beloved for one special night.

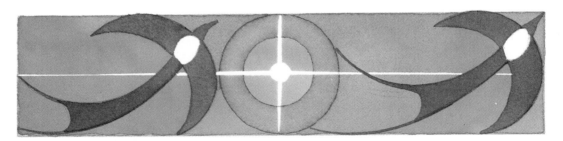

 *The Seventh Sister*—also know as *The Cowherd and the Spinning Maiden*—is a folktale from China. Chinese cultures have flourished since the earliest stages of human history. The Chinese people have invented many things we continue to use, such as paper, silk, and the compass.

China's population is now over one billion people, or nearly one-fifth of the world's total population. It is also one of the world's largest countries in land area. China has always been primarily an agricultural country. Grains, such as wheat and rice, are its major crops. The story of *The Seventh Sister* probably originated in the eastern lowlands, China's most productive farming area. Today's farmers still use oxen for plowing, much as Chang does in the story.

On the seventh day of the seventh month, the Chinese celebrate the Festival of the Milky Way. This is a special day in the lunar calendar, the traditional calendar of China that follows the complete phases of the moon. People hope for a clear night on this festival. According to tradition, if it rains, the magpies are washed away, and the tears of the Cowherd and Spinning Maiden fall to earth because they are separated for another year. Magpies, called the "happy bird," symbolize good luck. The Spinning Maiden herself is known as the goddess of weaving, and people look to her for help and skill in their handiwork. Most of all, *Chi Hsi* is a special day for lovers, similar to our Valentine's Day. The entire country celebrates the love that the Cowherd had for his Spinning Maiden.